Always,
Julia

Books by Marcia Wood

The Secret Life of Hilary Thorne
The Search for Jim McGwynn
Always, Julia

Always, Julia

by
Marcia Wood

Atheneum   1993   New York

Maxwell Macmillan Canada
Toronto

Maxwell Macmillan International
New York   Oxford   Singapore   Sydney

My thanks to Laurence Libin, Frederick P. Rose Curator of the Department of Musical Instruments, Metropolitan Museum of Art, for his correspondence regarding the luthier's workshop exhibit.

Atheneum
Macmillan Publishing Company
866 Third Avenue
New York, NY 10022

Maxwell Macmillan Canada, Inc.
1200 Eglinton Avenue East
Suite 200
Don Mills, Ontario M3C 3N1

Macmillan Publishing Company is part of the
Maxwell Communication Group of Companies.

First edition

Printed in the United States of America

10 9 8 7 6 5 4 3 2 1

The text of this book is set in 12 pt. DeVinne.

Book design by Kathryn Parise

LIBRARY OF CONGRESS CATALOGING-IN-PUBLICATION DATA

Wood, Marcia.
    Always, Julia/Marcia Wood.
        p.   cm.
    Summary: Jane's letters from her sister, Julia, an aspiring writer living in New York City, help Jane deal with the pressures of growing up.
    ISBN 0–689–31728–X
    [1. Sisters—Fiction.   2. Letters—Fiction.   3. Authorship—Fiction.   4. New York (N.Y.)—Fiction.]   1. Title.
PZ7.W8499A1   1993
[Fic]—dc20   91-40460

To Fred,
the star by which I set my course,
and to my own little sister, Nell,
who has been proud of me

This book exists because of you both

Chapter 1

The first letter came on my birthday.

It felt like springtime, even though the calendar did say January. On my way home from school I'd noticed that the dogwood trees and the red-bud looked about to bloom. The sidewalks had that wet, mossy smell. I remember once Julia said that springtime smelled like gunpowder. Once on a spring night she and a bunch of her friends went out to the river and jumped around on the old railroad bridge. The cops, when they got there, thought that all the kids were drunk or something, but they weren't, Julia said. They just felt like—exploding.

I wondered what springtime smelled like in New York, and if Julia still felt like exploding.

My mother had left the letter on the front hall

table for me. I took it up to my room and closed the
door.

Julia had been gone since Christmas.

Dear Janey:

I'm here, I'm here, I'M HERE!!

*Everything is fine. I've got a room at the
Chelsea Hotel, and I'm enrolled at City College.
All those honors classes I took in high school
finally paid off—I didn't have to take Fresh-
man English so I could get that seminar I
wanted with Nicholas Quill. You know—he
wrote* Tears in the Dust.

*The first class is tomorrow. I can hardly
wait! Do you realize—this, here, right now, is
the very beginning of everything for me. Now
I know how Pinocchio must have felt when he
was finally about to turn into a boy: Up to now
I've been just a collection of dreams and hopes
and maybes—but I'm about to turn into a person. I'm about to turn into myself. It makes
me feel solemn to think about it.*

Is Mother still angry?

*You know what she makes me think of? One
of those granite images that ancient primitive
tribes used to worship.*

*Actually I don't care whether she's mad at
me or not. I don't have to look at her across
the dinner table anymore. But one of these
days I'll come home, famous, respected, and*

world-renowned, and she'll have to say she was
wrong. I can't wait to see that stone face crack.
Happy Birthday, little sister!
Write soon. I love you—

Always,
Julia

I went downstairs to look for Mother, debating whether or not to tell her about Julia's letter. The whole subject of Julia was a delicate one, and the peace we'd built since she left was fragile.

Julia's the one who likes explosions—not me.

Mother was in her study, at her desk. Her smooth hair gleamed like burnished metal in the lamplight.

She glanced up when I knocked on the door frame and smiled. "Hello, darling. Have a nice day?"

"Yes," I said. "Some of the girls made me a cake. We had it in the cafeteria at lunchtime."

"How lovely!"

"Yes."

She looked at me. "Are you sorry now that you didn't want a birthday party?"

I shook my head. Fifteen is too much in the middle to have a birthday party—too old for some kinds of parties, too young for others. Besides, birthdays in our family have always had a tradition. We open presents in the morning at breakfast time, and we go to The Coach House Restaurant for dinner. We order prime rib and we have cheesecake for dessert. We've done this for as long as I can remember—even way back when Daddy was alive and I needed a booster seat to reach the table.

"I want the same kind of birthday we always have," I said.

"I'm afraid with only the two of us it won't be much of a celebration," she said. "Don't you want to bring a friend? How about Eben? I could ask Tom and we could make it a foursome—a double date. That would be fun, wouldn't it?"

A double date. It sounded sophisticated. Maybe they'd offer me a glass of wine, or maybe even a cocktail. "No," I said. "Birthdays are for family."

She sighed. "All right," she said. "I'll make the reservations."

It *was* my birthday, after all. On my birthday, at least, I ought to be able to have what I want.

Chapter 2

Julia loves to write letters.

Dear Janey:

If you ever came to New York, you'd never think you were on the same continent—or even on the same planet.

There's so much movement. That's the biggest thing. Crowds of people surge in tides along the streets. Lights flash. Whistles blow. Radios blare. Buildings go up and come down. Cars, buses, trucks, subways. Even the sidewalks tremble. Nothing ever stops moving.

There's so much to take in. Sometimes I think I can even see molecules spin....

Nicholas Quill is an interesting person. On one hand, he has eyes you could drown in—soft and warm and deep—but on the other

hand he seems kind of detached—reluctant to
get involved with people. The other day in
class one girl came in with one side of her face
all banged up. The one eye she could see out
of was positively naked—you could see all the
way down to the bottom of her, how hurt and
desperately afraid she was. She came into the
room with her head down and sat in the very
back as though to hide herself, but when Nicho-
las Quill was roaming around the room talking
about the difference between plot and theme,
he noticed her. His voice faltered and he
stopped. Then he stepped back, away from her,
and turned away. . . .

Today at school Mrs. Albright asked about her.

In humanities class we were talking about careers—Mrs. Albright said tenth grade was not too
early to begin to explore your options. She said that
most people don't have one particular, outstanding
talent that makes it easy to choose what to do with
their lives; most people have to search around to find
out what they're good at. Randy Gardiner raised his
hand and asked how we were supposed to search.
After all, he said, the only careers you usually know
anything about are the ones your parents or your
relatives have. That kind of limits your choices.

So Mrs. Albright assigned us a project. We each
have to pick a career—anything—and research it.
Then at the end of term we'll have a career fair—sit

in booths and pretend to have those careers so that other kids can ask us questions about our jobs and learn something.

I have no idea what career to pick.

After class Mrs. Albright called to me as the other kids were leaving the room. "Jane, how is Julia doing?"

"Okay," I said. "She's in New York now. She said the university here didn't have the writing courses she wanted."

Mrs. Albright nodded. "Well, I'm sure she knows what she's doing."

I nodded. A writer is the only thing Julia's ever wanted to be. In her room at home she used to have this giant poster called "Masters of American Literature." It was a whole collage of pictures of famous writers, and before she finished high school she'd read everything every one of them had ever written. Once for her birthday I cut up an old photograph and pasted her picture right next to F. Scott Fitzgerald's on the poster.

Julia would never have had a problem with this humanities project.

Mother wouldn't have, either.

"What a marvelous idea!" she exclaimed when I told her about the assignment. "It's about time they started you kids thinking ahead. What career are you going to pick?"

"I don't know yet," I said. "I can't really think of anything."

She immediately said, "You can do my career."

Mother's vice president of an insurance company. She started out as an actuary, which is something or other to do with statistics; I'm not sure just what.

I'm not crazy about math. Except for geometry; I like geometry. But I don't know. Mrs. Albright said we could do any career—it doesn't necessarily *have* to be one we would want for ourselves.

"Or, I'm sure Tom would be happy to talk to you, if you like," she offered.

Tom Easley is Mother's friend—she says "boyfriend" isn't dignified—and he's a publisher. He owns our town's only newspaper.

But I'm not crazy about English either, so the newspaper business isn't any better than insurance.

"Thanks, Mother," I said. "I'll think about it. I'm not sure yet what I want to do."

She frowned. "Well, for God's sake, do something practical. I don't need *both* my daughters starving to death."

I didn't want to listen to her talk about Julia, so I went downstairs to my workshop.

My workshop's my favorite place in the house. It's in a corner of the basement but there are two windows right there, and a door to the outside so it gets lots of light and air. My friend Eben and I put Peg-Board on the walls and fluorescent lights in the ceiling, and we built the workbenches ourselves. They—the workbenches—sit in a U-shape so I can be in the middle and reach all my tools and supplies. It's all just right—we even put rubber tiling on the floor to reduce fatigue. I keep it very neat so I always know exactly where everything is—it makes me feel good to see all my saws and drills and stuff ranged there just waiting for me to use them.

I make birdhouses.

Not to sell or anything; just for fun. I guess it started when I was a Girl Scout—I made one to get my woodworking badge. That first one was pretty simple: just four sides, a bottom, a roof, and a hole in the front—I didn't even paint it—but there was something that I really loved about making it. I liked sanding the wood and feeling how silky it could get; I liked hammering in the nails to make the corners sturdy. And then, when it was done, I liked the weight of it in my hands when I held it. It made me feel— satisfied.

I've made lots of birdhouses since then. Each one's been a little more complicated than the last—I get carried away sometimes. I just finished one that looks like Hänsel and Gretel's gingerbread cottage: I painted on a shingled roof, and shutters alongside the windows, and little curlicues around the door and on the corners.

I always put the birdhouses outside when I'm finished; Mother says our backyard is beginning to look like a bird-sized version of Disneyland. I know she'd like to have a more elegant-looking landscape around our house; but she hasn't actually *told* me to stop putting out my birdhouses, so I haven't.

I sat down at my bench and pulled out my scrapbook. It's a bunch of photographs and postcards and newspaper clippings about interesting-looking buildings. I keep it to look through whenever I need an idea for a new project.

There's a house in California somewhere that's supposed to have a hundred rooms. An old lady built it to make room for all the ghosts she thought were haunting her—I'd like to build a copy of that house someday. And the Taj Mahal—I'd like to do that too. It might be interesting to make that onion-shaped roof.

I was trying to think how to do it when there was a knock on the basement door. I looked up; it was Eben. He often came over if he saw my workshop lights on. I reached over and unlatched the door.

"Eben," I said, "do you think, if I carved this roof out of a solid piece of wood, that the walls would be strong enough to hold it up?" I showed him the picture of the Taj.

He studied it, leaning his shoulders against the door frame and raking his dark hair out of his eyes with his hand. Mother thinks Eben's hair is too long— shaggy she calls it. But I think looking rumpled suits him. Eben is the most relaxed, comfortable person I know.

"I think so," he said, handing me back the picture. "If you make it out of some really lightweight wood. And if you brace the walls."

I've known Eben all my life. He lives next door. He was in Julia's class at school, but he's always been

10

more my friend than Julia's—I guess because he's a year younger than Ju. He goes to the university right here in town—where Julia was until she ran away—so he's still living at home and I still get to see him a lot. Which is especially good because Eben is studying to be an architect and he knows a lot that can help me with my birdhouses.

Eben said abruptly, "Is something bothering you?"

I stared at him. "What do you mean?"

"You always come down here to hide out. I thought maybe something was wrong."

I shrugged. "Nothing monumental."

"Are you still upset about Julia?" he asked. "Janeybird, you knew she was going to leave home someday."

He ran a finger lightly across my hand. It gave me the shivers and I pulled my hand away. Eben and I used to be pals; we didn't think about each other *that* way. But now—

Why do things have to change?

"It's not just Julia." It almost burst out of me. "It's *everything*! In school they're making us think about *careers*, and you—"

"Me what?"

"You're different."

"Different how?"

"I don't know." I didn't know the words to explain how I felt. I just had this feeling that Eben wanted to—I don't know—

I felt afraid.

"Maybe it's because you're in college now," I said.

He put his hand over mine. "Janeybird, you're still my best friend."

"I know," I said helplessly.

"I would never hurt you," he said gently.

"I know," I repeated.

I did. I trusted Eben. But still.

When I was little it used to seem to me that days were like stepping stones—you stepped from one round, even pretty stone to the next, all the way down the path. You could see all the stones, just alike, that lay in front of you. You knew what was in store. You knew, for instance, what fourth grade would be like when you were still in third: You knew Miss Harris would take you to the museum to see the mummy, and you knew that you'd start fractions in math class. And you knew before you got there what junior high would be like, and when you got to junior high you knew the way high school would be. When you're little, you know things.

But now I feel like there isn't any path. I can't see where to go.

I miss Julia.

Chapter 3

Dear Janey,

Nicholas Quill thinks I'm promising!

Last week we had to write a character sketch—I did him!—and we got them back today. "A promising beginning," he said.

Promising!

I'm so excited! What a wonderful thing for him to say! What a wonderful thing to be! Promising! Don't you think it sounds like an egg about to hatch, or a flower—no, wait, I know—it sounds like the rev of a jet just about to soar into the sky!

Promising!

I am so glad I came here.

But I'm not going to let it go to my head. Since it's probably going to be awhile before I fulfill my promise (oh I get a chill inside *whenever I say the word!), the next thing I'm going to do is look for a job, to help stretch the money from Daddy's insurance. You have no idea how expensive it is to live here. And maybe I can find an apartment to share or something—this hotel is pretty extravagant—but oh, Janey, do you realize what I'm doing? I'm actually living where Thomas Wolfe once did! Sometimes in the corridors I can hear the sound of a typewriter and I imagine that it's his; I imagine that I'm actually there, in 1930. We're going to have lunch at the Algonquin, I think, and we'll meet Hemingway for cocktails. . . .*

I heard Mother hang up the phone in the front hall and come partway up the stairs. "Jane? Tom and I are going to The Greenhouse for something to eat. Do you want to come?"

I had to study for a test, and I wanted to do some work on my Taj Mahal. "No, thanks. I'll make a sandwich or something."

She came up the rest of the way and stood in the doorway of my room. Her earrings glinted sharply in the rays of the setting sun through my window. "I wish you would, dear."

Why did she ask me if I *wanted* to come, if she was going to *make* me come whether I wanted to or not?

"You could ask him about your career project,"

Mother added, persuasively. "And we'll be home early."

I felt that pressure inside, that I always get when she tries to steer me. I always feel as though I have to do what she wants me to do, because if I say no she'll explode into a thunderstorm of wrath.

"Mother," I said. My voice only shook a little. "I'm not ready to start on my career project. I've told you that. And I don't want to go out for dinner. I have homework to do, and I want to work on my birdhouse."

She was silent for a moment, then she said, "All right, dear. I'll see you when I get home, then. Have a good evening." She turned away and went back down the stairs. I heard the front door open and close, and she was gone.

For a minute I was too surprised to move.

Nothing bad had happened.

But, after all, all I wanted to do was have dinner at home. I didn't want to leave the university, take all my inheritance out of the bank and move to New York.

Still. Mother liked her daughters to do things her way. And this time, I did it my way.

Like Ju, sort of.

I felt proud of myself. Elated. Jumpy. Since I couldn't sit still, I went downstairs to my workshop.

I was using balsa wood to build my little Taj, and balsa's so soft and porous you can make scratches on it with just the point of a pin. So, instead of painting on all the little carvings and decorations that cover the walls of the Taj, I thought I'd try to carve them in.

I took a piece of scrap wood and made a few experimental marks, lines and curves and circles. It seemed to work all right. Then I got a piece of tracing paper and copied out part of the design on the wall from the picture of the Taj. I copied that with carbon paper onto my scrap wood and then I went over those lines with my pin to make the carvings. The pin worked okay, but the carbon paper left blue lines in the wood that I couldn't rub out. I tried just to copy the design freehand onto the wood with my pin but that didn't work. It's hard to draw with a pin.

There was a knock at the basement door. Eben.

"Eben, what am I going to do? The carbon paper leaves blue lines and I don't know how else to get the design on the wood!" I was so glad to see him I forgot about how awkward our last conversation was.

Eben looked at my experiment. He was just as comfortable as always. Liking for him welled up inside of me.

"But you don't need to worry about the lines," he said. "Look, I'll show you. Got any stain?"

I handed him a bottle of stain and a rag. He tipped some stain onto the rag and wiped it over my carvings. The dents that I'd made got much darker than the rest of the wood. They looked like very deep etchings, and the blue tracings were completely covered over.

"You did a good job on this," he said. "What made you think of doing it this way?"

"I don't know," I said. "I just wanted to make it look more real."

"Looks good," he said.

As he tossed the rag onto the bench I caught sight of his watch. "Eleven o'clock!" I gasped. "How can it be so late?"

He laughed at me. "Time marches, Janeybird."

"But Mother was supposed to be home hours ago! Do you suppose something's happened to her?"

"She is home," said Eben. "At least, her car's in the driveway and the light in her bedroom is on. I saw it when I was coming over."

"Oh," I said blankly. I hadn't even heard her come in.

"Just like Julia," Eben teased. "When you're doing what you like, you don't think about anything else."

"Oh, *no*!" I said, remembering. "I have a biology test tomorrow and I haven't even opened the book!"

Chapter 4

Valentine's Day. There was a dance at school but I wasn't really interested. I'm not crazy about big crowds of people. My idea of a good time is working on my birdhouses, or going out for ice cream with Eben, or something like that. Kid stuff. Maybe I'll never be a grown-up.

There was a letter from Julia when I got home, of course. She's written almost every day.

But this letter was special.

Dear Janey:

I sent a short story I did for Nicholas Quill's class to a magazine—the Northeastern Review, *and guess what?*

They're going to publish it!

I'm not sure when—their letter didn't say—I guess the whole process takes a long time and it could be a year, or maybe even more, before it actually gets in print, but the main thing is that they are going to publish it!

It was so funny—I got the letter when I got back to the hotel the night before last, so yesterday in class was the first chance I got to tell anybody who would really understand what it meant, so when I got to class and my friend Rosie was sitting there I just grabbed her by the arm and I said, "They liked it! They liked it!" She said, "What? Who did?" "My story! Northeastern Review! *They're going to publish it!" She screamed with me, and we danced around the room liked lunatics holding on to one another and laughing—then Nicholas Quill came into the room and we told him and he smiled. . . .*

Tom had dinner with us that night.

I like Tom. He thinks my birdhouses are neat. Whenever he goes on a business trip he brings me back postcards of interesting buildings for my scrapbook.

Mother brought the casserole into the dining room, and when everyone was sitting down, I said, "Mother, I got a letter from Julia today."

Mother cut her salad carefully with the side of her fork and said in a polite voice, "Did you?"

I waited, but she didn't say anything else so I went on. "She's sold her first story!"

20

"Tom," said Mother, "do you know where our seats are at the play tonight?"

Tom shot a glance at her, but replied calmly, "We've got our usual pair."

"I'm so glad," said Mother. "There are so few good seats at the University Theatre. I don't know why they don't raze it and build a new one."

"Undoubtedly they're waiting for a bequest. As a matter of fact," he said, "I hear there's one about to be announced."

Mother shook her head. "You newspaper people. Is there anything you don't find out?"

Tom spread his hands. "What can I say? The nose for news is an occupational hazard."

I said loudly, "She's got a place to stay, and she's in school and she's taking a seminar with Nicholas Quill, the famous author!"

"Jane, please," said my mother.

"You were wrong about how terrible her life would be," I said.

Mother and Julia had argued over Julia being a writer for as long as I could remember. They were both terrifically stubborn, and neither one of them would give an inch—Julia was always excited, frolicking around like a kite in the wind, and Mother was always jerking the string, trying to get her down to earth. Julia, being Julia, flew higher the harder Mother tugged. Once Julia was all worked up because she'd just won a prize for a poem that she'd written. The poem had been about Christmas dinner, so now

21

Ju thought maybe she'd work on a whole book of poems all about food.

Her eyes gleamed at the thought. "Think about it, Janey—maybe I could even hook up with a cookbook writer or a chef or something and do a book of poems and recipes. *Food for Body and Soul*, we could call it."

Unfortunately that night we had meat loaf and string beans for dinner. Julia had to struggle to find something soulful to say about meat loaf. At the table she poked at her meal with her fork and mused aloud.

"What does meat loaf represent to you, Janey? What does it make you think of?"

I stared down at my plate. I wasn't sure what she wanted, but I wanted to help. "It's not too bad with gravy on it," I said finally.

"But how does it make you *feel*? Does it make you feel warm and safe and cuddled, or do you feel like you're being punished for something? Some people hate meat loaf," she added in a conversational tone.

My mother cut in. "It *should* make you feel grateful that there's a meal on the table."

Julia waved it away. "Oh, Mother, there's more to life than meals."

"Try to do without them then," Mother said crisply.

Julia sighed. "Oh, Mother, why are you so *literal*?"

"And why are *you* so impractical? Cookbook poetry indeed," my mother said in a disgusted voice.

22

"How many meals do you think that will put on your table? Julia, it's past time that you started thinking of your future."

"I *am* thinking of the future, Mother!"

"Oh? How do you plan to make a living?"

"By writing," Julia said coolly.

Mother snorted.

Julia flushed. "*Some* people think I'm talented, Mother."

Mother said, "Be sensible, Julia. The average writer makes less than four thousand dollars a year from writing. You have to have another way to support yourself."

Julia pushed back her chair and stood up. "Mother, why do you think I can't make a success of this? Do you think I'm only average?"

Mother sighed. "Don't be ridiculous, Julia."

The memory of all this flashed across my mind as I announced Julia's good news. Mother would hate being proved wrong, I was sure. I waited for the storm to break over my head.

But all she said was, "Jane, have you talked to Tom about your career project?"

To Tom she said, "Jane thinks she may want to go into newspaper publishing."

I don't know what made me angrier—that she was ignoring Julia's news, or that she'd decided the rest of my life for me. "Mother, I do not! With my grades in English how could you possibly think I'd be interested in journalism?"

"Your grades would be fine if you applied yourself," she said tartly.

"But I don't want to apply myself! Mother, I'm not interested!"

Mother folded her napkin carefully and put it on the table next to her plate. "You're going into some sort of practical career, Jane. Make up your mind to that now. I don't want any more foolishness when your turn comes. Coffee, Tom?" She rose from her chair and went out to the kitchen.

I shouted at her back, "You were wrong about Julia! What makes you think you'd be right about me?" I shoved back my chair and stalked out of the dining room.

"Jane."

Tom had followed me out of the living room and was standing at the foot of the stairs. I could see the little bald spot in his curly blond hair. I liked him for it; my mother had been dyeing the gray out of her hair for as long as I could remember.

Tom was so—*clear.* You could see what he was like and what he thought just by looking at him. For the ten millionth time I wondered about him and my mother together. They were so opposite.

"Try not to think too badly of your mother," he said.

"How can you stand to come around here?" I exclaimed. "She's a cold, hard woman! A statue!"

Tom put his hands in his pockets and leaned

against the banister with a thoughtful air. "She's not cold, really," he said slowly. "She has her pride, I grant you, but I don't think she's cold. Cold people don't get angry."

Maybe she puts on a different face for him when they're alone, I thought. That wouldn't be beyond her. But how can he not see through that?

Of course, Tom probably just assumes everyone is just as happy and easy as he is himself. Probably his whole family is like that. What could he know about people like my mother?

"Your mother is a rare human being," he said quietly.

"I know, I know. It wasn't easy for her when my father died," I recited in a singsong voice. "She went back to school, graduated in double-quick time, found a job, and went to work, all with two small children to be responsible for." All my life people had been telling me what a wonderful person my mother was. And it's not that I don't appreciate it—

But I wanted to make him see what it was like for me. "But she doesn't care what *we* want; she only cares about making us just like her!"

"No, she *doesn't* want you to be like her. Have you thought of that?"

I didn't know what he meant.

"Tom!" My mother's voice floated into the hall. "We should go."

"I'm ready!" Tom called out. He turned back to

me. "Jane, please? I'm not asking you to agree with her, just try to understand her. Think about it?" He ran down the steps to rejoin my mother.

I went downstairs to the workshop. My little Taj was almost finished. All I had to do was make a base for it to sit on. The real Taj Mahal sits in the middle of a marble-tiled courtyard so I thought I'd try to make a base that looked like that.

What I'd like to do someday is build a whole little miniature town. A town where everyone would fit. Build a house for Julia with a room full of windows where she could write her books. Build a bookshop too to sell them. My friend Denise has always said she'd like to own a bookshop, so she could live there too. Eben could be the town architect. He could design all the buildings—he could design a skyscraper for Mother where she could have her office on the top floor.

Later that evening I told Eben about my town while we were eating hot fudge sundaes at Baskin-Robbins.

"Your dad can be the doctor in my town," I said. "I like your dad."

Eben laughed. "Are you only going to have people you like in your town?"

"Yes! Why should I build a town for people I don't like?"

Eben said teasingly, "I don't think my dad would come without my mom. Will you let her in?"

"Yeah. I like her. She can be—" I stopped to think.

Eben's mother is an architect and my town already had one of those.

"Let her play the flute with the symphony," Eben said. "She told me once she always wished that she could play the flute."

"Okay," I said, "but we don't have a symphony hall. We'll have to build one."

"Where are we going to get the money for a symphony hall?"

I hadn't thought of that.

Eben began to laugh. "You look so worried!"

Then I began to laugh too. Then Eben laughed even harder. He had tears streaming down his face and I was choking on my ice cream. Everybody in the place was looking at us, but we didn't care.

Finally I cleaned off my face. "It all seemed so real!" I said.

"Yeah," he said, wiping his eyes. "I wish we could do it."

"Maybe someday some long-lost uncle will leave us an island or something for us to build our town on."

"Or maybe Julia will get so rich and famous she'll buy us one."

"Or maybe we'll get rich and famous!"

"Architects get gold medals for their best efforts; they don't get rich and famous," said Eben. "So it's got to be either you or Julia."

"Since I can't even come up with a project for the career fair," I said, "I guess our best chance is Julia."

* * *

I remember something else about the night of the Great Meat Loaf Fight. Later that evening, when I went upstairs, I saw Julia through the open door of her room. She'd shoved her notebook and papers off her desk and buried her head in her arms. I could hear her sobbing.

Julia cries often. More often than most people. Mother calls it "theatrical emotionalism." But I don't know—I suppose artistic people do feel things, good and bad, more acutely than other people. I guess that's part of what makes them able to show things to the rest of us. Julia told me once that writing a story is like building an iceberg—in order for the iceberg to be seen on top of the water, there has to be all that unseen stuff underneath.

When I see Julia cry, or get into one of those piano-wire-tight giggly moods of hers, I almost feel glad I'm a drone.

I knew from experience that soon she'd stop crying. But then she'd start thinking over again about what Mother had said, and then she'd get angry. Julia throws things when she's angry. Some of them hurt. I moved out of the line of fire.

Anyone who felt as deeply as Julia, I thought, must be destined for great things. Someday, I knew, she'd have everything she dreamed of. Someday she'd help Eben and me build our town

Chapter 5

I varnished my Taj to make it gleam the way the real one did, then I put it in the front yard, on top of the sundial, to let it dry. I couldn't put it in the backyard because there wasn't anything out there to set it on, so I just hoped Mother wouldn't mind it out front for a few hours.

I thought it looked nice.

The mailman liked it too. When he handed me the mail he said, "That's too beautiful to be a dirty old birdhouse, Jane; it ought to go in a museum."

I thanked him and looked through the letters.

Dear Jane:

Guess what?

Last night Rosie and I went to a party with some people she knows—it was just the way I always dreamed New York would be. There were editors there, and agents, and writers, and even some actors and I saw some TV people too—Rosie's dad works for Time *so she knows lots of people like that. And of course I'm not shy—we sailed through the evening, laughing and joking and chatting to people as though we went to 100-watt parties every night.*

Rosie told everyone about my story. Everybody was interested—people were so nice. The baby star, they called me. I felt like a kitten taking a bath in cream. One guy said he could send my story to someone in Hollywood! My story—my very first story—a movie!

The doorbell rang and I went to answer it. It was a woman I didn't know; there was a car at the curb.

"Hello," she said. "I hope I'm not disturbing you; I was driving past and my eye was caught by that model there." She nodded her head toward my Taj.

I was puzzled. "My birdhouse?"

She handed me a business card. ANNE OWENS, it said. MISSOURI STATE LIBRARY. "I promise you I'm not a vandal," she said. Her dark eyes beamed with friendliness and humor. "Can I take a closer look at it?"

I hesitated. Nobody was home but me, so I wasn't too keen on consorting with a stranger. But—somebody interested in my birdhouse!

Eben's mother's car was in their driveway. She'd hear me yell, if we stayed outside. "Okay," I said.

I walked across the grass with her. "You said 'your birdhouse,' " she said. "Did you build it?"

"Yes," I said.

She knelt down by the Taj. "How did you make these spires? And these balusters? They're so small, and yet they're perfectly tapered."

"They're toothpicks," I said. "I just cut them to the length I wanted."

"And this courtyard. It looks like marble, but surely it isn't?"

I grinned. "No. I got a sheet of clear acrylic and painted with two colors on the underside. I hoped that when you looked through the acrylic at the paint it would look like marble, all deep-colored and shiny."

"You were right." She straightened up. "And you did this all yourself?"

"Pretty much," I answered. "My friend Eben gave me some ideas."

"It's a beautiful piece of work," the woman said. "You're very talented."

Talented. My face started to tingle.

"I wonder if you'd allow us to borrow it," she continued. "We're trying to put together a display of Young Missouri Artists at the capitol. We'd love to have this."

I must have looked like I don't know what. "You mean you think I'm a young Missouri artist?"

31

"I don't think it, I know it," said the woman, laughing.

"But it's just a birdhouse!"

"You can call it a birdhouse if you like," the woman said. "I call it extraordinary."

She asked me for my name and phone number, and said she'd be in touch within a couple of weeks. She said if my parents had any questions about insurance or security concerning the exhibit they should call her.

"And take it inside, for heaven's sake," she called back as she got into the car. "Don't let it get rained on!"

Chapter 6

Dear Jane:

Did you notice my new address? Rosie and I have decided to share an apartment, so from now on write to me there. I'll send you the phone number when we get one installed. Here in New York it takes months to get a phone, usually because somebody or other is on strike.

It's a great place—we're subletting it from a friend of her dad's who's going to be living in Europe for a year. All the doorways are arches, and all the floors are little squares of parquet. The rooms are big and the ceilings are high and the building is elegant—and the furniture—it belongs to the guy in Europe—is luxurious and expensive and comfortable— just exactly, in fact, what I would have chosen myself! You'd love to make a birdhouse of it!

*Nicholas Quill says that for our final proj-
ect in the seminar we're to submit the outline
of a novel. I have the perfect idea, but I won't
tell you what it is because I want you to be
surprised . . .*

I was hurt, a little. Ju hadn't said anything about
my Taj, which I'd written her about right on that
first day Anne Owens came by. Then I thought,
maybe that's the surprise. Maybe she's going to write
about me. Still, it didn't seem like Julia not to say
something about my good news. Of course, I didn't
know what did seem "like" Julia now that she was
more than—what had she said?—"dreams and hopes
and maybes." She must be awfully busy. Maybe she
hasn't even gotten my letter yet.

Anyway I was glad for her.

I heard the garage door open, and Mother's car
drive in. I went to the door to meet her.

"Well?" I asked her before she'd even put down
her briefcase. "Did you talk to him? What did he say?"

Mother had been going to check with Tom about
Anne Owens and the Missouri State Library and the
exhibit. Neither of us had ever heard of a state library, so Mother thought it would be a good idea to
verify it before I got my hopes up.

She smiled. "Apparently it's quite legitimate," she
said. "Ms. Owens is everything—and more—that she
said she was. Those exhibits she puts on in the state

capitol receive national attention." She stretched out an arm to hug my shoulders. "Congratulations, Jane!"

I'd been afraid to get too excited about the whole thing, because when I'd told Mother about Ms. Owens she'd been all cautious and doubtful, but now it was okay to get excited and I could hardly take it in. National attention!

"There will probably be some sort of reception on the opening night of the exhibit. I understand that's how it's usually done," Mother said. "And sometimes the governor attends. This is quite an honor, dear."

"I guess." I could barely sit still; I felt like someone had pulled a cord and sent me spinning off into the air.

"Did she say when the exhibit would be?"

"She said she'd write us all the details."

"We'll go together," my mother said, "and we can ask Eben too, if you like. And I'm sure Tom would like to be there. Maybe you'll get your picture in the paper."

"Oh," I said, "it's probably not that big a deal."

"But it is," she insisted. "Tom said all the papers in the state cover these exhibits."

"Well ... " My voice trailed off.

"I'm proud of you, Jane," said my mother.

I couldn't remember a time when she'd ever said that before, either to Julia or me.

"I remember being your age," she went on. "I would have died in ecstasy if one of my watercolors had ever been chosen for a show. For a while I entered every competition I could find. But nothing ever came of it."

She moved to the front hall mirror, inspected herself critically, smoothed a recalcitrant hair.

I hadn't known my mother ever painted.

Chapter 7

On Thursday I stayed late in art class because the spray booth had been busy all period and I'd wanted to put fixative on the charcoal sketch I'd done for Julia's birthday. I slipped into humanities class just as Mrs. Albright was passing out sheets of paper.

"—and I must have these back, signed by a parent, no later than March fifteenth—two weeks from to-day—if you want to go," she was saying. "Don't worry about the deposit by that date—we just need a head count for airline reservations and hotel rooms."

Airline reservations and hotel rooms?

I leaned over to nudge Randy Gardiner. "What's going on?"

"A trip to New York during spring vacation," he said. "To see plays and museums and stuff."

New York!

Julia!

She'd always said she wouldn't come home till she was famous, but I could go see her!

If—

I raised my hand. "When's spring vacation this year?"

"The last week in April. If you'd been on time, Jane, you would have heard me say so." Mrs. Albright never appreciated tardiness.

"Sorry." That was okay, then. The exhibit didn't open until the end of May. I could do both.

If Mother approved.

And if Julia was going to *be* in New York during that week. Her last letter had been full of plans to maybe go out to Hollywood and talk to someone about her story. Julia thought maybe a TV movie would be better than a theatrical release—actually, she said, what she'd really like best was if "Masterpiece Theatre" did something with it.

I still hadn't read the story. I'd asked her a couple of times to send me a copy but I guess it's hard to remember niggling little things like that when you have publishing contracts and movie deals to think about.

I waited until the weekend to broach it with Mother.

Saturday's the only day she really relaxes in the morning. She has a second cup of coffee and reads the paper, then we usually talk for a while about what we want to get done over the weekend. She likes to do stuff around the house on Saturdays. Since that's the kind of stuff I like to do too, we're usually in pretty good moods on Saturdays. Unless she wants to go shopping or something, in which case I'm in a lousy mood if she wants me to go with her.

"Oh, look," she said at the breakfast table. "They're going to bring the national touring company of *Starlight Express* to the University Theater. I'd love to see that, wouldn't you?"

I blinked. "Isn't that the one they do on roller skates?" I asked. "That doesn't seem like your style."

Mother smiled almost sheepishly. "Well, I'd just like to see how it's done."

"Speaking of theater," I said, "you know my humanities teacher, Mrs. Albright? She's taking a bunch of kids to New York over spring vacation. To go to plays and stuff."

"I like that Mrs. Albright," said Mother. "She really tries to expand your horizons. By the way, how's that career project going? Any ideas yet?"

"No." I glossed over that in a hurry. "So maybe you'd let me go to New York?"

"Perhaps. I'd like to see how much it costs, and what the chaperoning arrangements are, and that sort of thing, but it doesn't seem totally out of the question."

I threw my arms around her neck and kissed her, which made *her* blink. "Oh, Mother—Mom—you're great!" Then I ran upstairs to write to Julia.

If I mail this today, I calculated, she'll get it by Wednesday, and I'll get her answer next Saturday. I crammed the letter in an envelope and slapped a stamp on just as the mailman started up our walk. I got it down to him in the nick and he took it away, and then I relaxed and sat back to wait for Julia's answer.

But it never came.

Chapter 8

At first I wasn't too worried when I didn't hear back from Julia right away. After all, the mail could have been delayed, or Julia could have been busy, or out of town or something—maybe even in Hollywood about the movie from her story. I was just going to have to get used to having a famous sister.

But the days went by, and still I didn't hear anything. And I realized that Julia had never sent me her phone number. I called directory assistance in New York City, but they didn't have a listing for her.

Somehow, up until then, Julia's letters had made her seem so close I hadn't really thought about how far away New York City was. A different world, she had said. How different?

Two weeks went by and there wasn't any word.

"Mother," I said, "Julia hasn't written to me since I told her I was coming to New York."

It was Monday morning. We were in the car; Mother was going to drop me off at school on her way to work. She looked perfect, like an orchid in a florist's chilled case. She always looked especially elegant on Monday.

"Well, I imagine she's busy," Mother replied. She didn't take her eyes off the road.

"Too busy to write to me?"

"Jane, things change as you grow older and you have more responsibilities. She has more things to occupy her attention, that's all."

I felt sulky. "Maybe I shouldn't go see her at all then, if she's so busy," I said.

"Jane, don't be childish."

As the days went by with no letters from her I felt restless, frustrated. Not even my birdhouses could interest me.

I read Julia's old letters over and over again. There was one in particular—

... Yesterday I decided to go to the aquarium to soothe my mind. They have walking paths there that look out over the harbor; you can watch the ships come in and imagine where they've been—

I like to walk in New York. It helps me untangle problems, I think because the thoughts in my head fall into pattern with the rhythm of my feet. When words make a pattern, they make sense.

Anyway. Yesterday was a gray, cold day, so the aquarium was practically deserted. I looked into some of their outdoor pools but I guess it was even too crummy out for fish because all I saw was murky brown water. I was walking away from one of the pools, when BOOF! something hit me in the back—

I spun around and there was a yellow rubber beach ball rolling away down the sidewalk. I picked it up, looked around—there was no one in sight—then POMP! another beach ball, a blue one, sailed through the air and landed at my feet. I looked back at the murky pool just in time to see a dolphin's tail flip back under the water—

I ran back to the poolside. A dolphin face peered up at mine. "Did you throw that ball at me?" He made a short circle and came back around in front of me like a puppy.

I threw one of the balls back into the pool. He stopped it with the side of his nose and batted it right back at me—I threw it again— this time he had to swim for it but he got there and sent the ball flying again—

"Oh, yeah?" This time I threw both balls into the pool. My dolphin got one ball and

another dolphin appeared from nowhere to get
the other. And they laughed—I guess it was a
joke they often played—

Mother was wrong: Julia could never have gotten cold and hard, like her.

But I wondered: Why did Julia's mind need soothing?

The date for our trip seemed endlessly far away.

Sunday afternoon I went outside to plant some seedlings Mother had bought at a nursery sale. She liked to look out the window and see flowers, but she didn't like to work in the garden. I did, so the planting was my job.

It was a nice day. The sunshine had a delicate, fresh color, and it had rained the night before so everything smelled good. And Mother had bought lots of dianthus, my favorite flowers.

It felt good to dig in the dirt. I was about halfway finished when Eben wandered over.

"Want some help?"

"Sure." I handed him a trowel.

Eben has an eye for color. He put some of the bright red dianthus right in front of the larkspur, which is purple. I never would have thought of it, but I had to admit it looked good.

After we were done I went in and got a pitcher of lemonade and brought it back outside so we could admire our work while we rested.

He stretched out on the grass and shaded his eyes from the sun. "Ah, rest! You work me too hard, Janeybird."

I felt full of peace, comforted by the flowers and the dirt and the sunshine, golden now. "Don't you think we're a good team?" I asked. "Somehow everything always seems easier when you're there."

"Mmm." After a pause he said, "Are you busy next weekend?"

"No," I said. "Why?"

"There's a thing at school. A treasure hunt. I thought you might like to go."

"Oh." I envisioned crowds of people. Some of my contentment drained away. "No, I don't think so."

"It's not going to be big crowds of people, you know," he said. "You work in pairs, collecting clues and deciphering them. You have all weekend. The only time everybody comes together is at the end, to see who found the treasure. There's a party after that, but we wouldn't have to go." He grinned. "Unless we win."

"No, I don't think so," I repeated. That scared feeling was building up in me again. I wasn't sure I wanted to go to the places Eben wanted to take me.

"Why not?"

I shrugged.

"Janeybird, please go with me." He reached for my hand.

I pulled away.

His voice changed. "Jane. All I'm asking you is

to go somewhere I think you'll enjoy. I think I would enjoy it and I want to share it with you. Why won't you come?"

I shook my head.

"Jane. Do you realize that the only things we ever do together are the things *you* want to do? We work on *your* birdhouses; we go the places *you* want to go; we plant *your* flowers—"

"I thought you liked that!"

"I *do* like it! All I'm saying is that there are other things I like too, and I'd like to share them with you. But you don't seem to trust me."

"It isn't that!"

"Then what is it?"

I couldn't answer him. It was words that were the problem; I didn't have them. Even the thought of trying to describe how I felt made me feel all red.

"I just don't want to," I said feebly.

Eben sighed impatiently and got to his feet. "Well, when you grow up, you call me," he said, and walked away.

I went over to the corner of the yard and sat on the swing.

Chapter 9

I leaned across Randy Gardiner in the seat next to me to look out the window. The plane banked for a turn, and tiny lights blossomed like wildflowers in the darkness beneath us.

I'd never flown before. I knew what to expect, though, because Julia had written me about it.

> ... I'd thought that flying—even in a plane—would feel like a release. I thought I'd know how a porpoise feels when he bursts into the sky through the surface of the sea—but instead as we ascended I felt as though the heel of a giant hand were pressing me down into my seat, holding me still, keeping me back. What a disappointment. Just when you think you're going to break loose....

The whine of the engines tightened and then with a small, insignificant bump we were on the ground.

I don't know which rumbled more, the plane or my stomach. It felt like stage fright, kind of. Anticipation, I guess. I wasn't the only one either. All around the cabin passengers were moving restlessly, collecting their belongings, edging off their seats, ready to spring through the door and be on their way at the first possible moment.

Mrs. Albright, though, stayed relaxed and in her seat. She laughed at me when she saw my anxiety to be up and away. "Even if we're the last off the plane," she said, "we'll still have to wait for our luggage to be unloaded, so why push and be pushed?"

So I sat where I was and watched the column of people press by.

There were only seven of us on this trip—five students, Mrs. Albright, and Mr. Binkowski, the history teacher. Most parents hadn't been all that keen on sending their kids to New York for a week; Mother, of course, had thought that it was a marvelous idea. She hoped the trip would polish me.

"The theater, ballet, the symphony—Jane, what an opportunity!" she'd said when I'd given her the permission forms. "And the museums! Do you know, I was nearly thirty before I had a chance to see New York."

"You weren't so hot on Julia seeing New York," I'd muttered under my breath.

Of course she'd heard me. "These are entirely different circumstances," she'd replied coldly. "You are going to New York for a limited period of time, with adults, not running away to something you think of as the Emerald City."

The whole time before the trip I'd expected her to say something about Julia—give me a message for her, or maybe even forbid me to see her lest I be "influenced" or something, but she didn't. She'd never said a word about it.

Finally the plane emptied, and we got out of our seats and collected our belongings. The baggage was just coming onto the carousel when we got there; we picked up our luggage and got a taxi without the least problem. Everything was so easy; I'd expected there to be big crowds and lots of tension but there wasn't. It wasn't like I thought New York would be at all.

Mrs. Albright said, "We're not in New York yet, Jane. The airport's in New Jersey, remember?"

"That's right," I said, "we have to go through a tunnel." I remembered Julia's description.

> . . . *The city's an island, did you know that? You have to use either a tunnel or a bridge to get in—it's like going through the gates to Oz—*
>
> *I took the bus from the airport. I could see the city across the river—the afternoon sun*

49

*on the granite walls and windows of the sky-
scrapers made New York look all made of marble and gold—*

*The road into the city makes a great sweep-
ing dramatic loop before it plunges down into
thick yellow darkness—a tunnel. It smells bad
in the tunnel—like brimstone I think—but
before I can figure out how to get the window
closed we're out of the tunnel into a shock of
daylight. Then back into the darkness again,
into the Port Authority building, but now instead of going down we drive UP steep, angled
ramps—the bus groans with the strain.
Squares of daylight flash temptingly past the
windows. I begin to think there will always be
a pane of glass between me and New York.
And then, at last, at the top of the very last
ramp, the bus stops, and sets down all its passengers. . . .*

Of course, it was nighttime now, but everything
else was the same. As the taxi took us through the
tunnel Nella Cooper wrinkled up her nose and cried,
"Ew, what's that smell?"

"Julia says it's brimstone," I said.

Mr. Binkowski laughed.

We got to our hotel and checked in—the girls and
Mrs. Albright in one room and the guys and Mr.
Binkowski in another.

There were four of us in our room, but actually

there was plenty of space. The room was big, and the hotel people brought in cots so we each had our own bed. And there were two sinks in the bathroom. Mrs. Albright told us to unpack all our stuff and put it in the drawers and the closets so we wouldn't be tripping all over suitcases.

"And after all," she added, "I don't expect we'll be spending all that much time in the room."

She told us some of the stuff she had planned for us to do: go to the Metropolitan Museum, and the Whitney, and the Cooper-Hewitt; go to the Statue of Liberty, and the Empire State Building, and Radio City Music Hall; go see the ballet, and the symphony, and the theater; visit Central Park, and the Cloisters, and St. Patrick's Cathedral. Take a boat trip around Manhattan Island, and have tea at the Plaza. Shop on Fifth Avenue. The list was so long we began to laugh every time she added something else to it. She was right; we wouldn't be spending much time in our room.

But it made me wonder how much time I'd get to spend with Julia.

When the other girls went next door to see how the guys were settling in, I lingered.

"Mrs. Albright? Do all of us have to do everything on your list?"

She looked at me curiously. "What is it, Jane?"

"I was hoping I'd get to see Julia."

"But of course!" Mrs. Albright exclaimed. "Of course you can visit your sister! I'd like to see her too; perhaps she'll have dinner with us once or twice. What plans have you made with her?"

"Well, none, yet," I said. "I wrote to tell her when I'd be in New York, but I guess there wasn't time for her to write back. I have her address, though. I thought maybe I could go over to her apartment tomorrow."

"Certainly. Let's see." She thought a minute. "We're going to see the Statue of Liberty tomorrow morning, and to the theater tomorrow night, so how about tomorrow afternoon?"

"Perfect," I answered gratefully.

"Just one thing. Would it spoil your reunion if I went along with you? I'd much prefer that none of you kids wanders around the city alone. Mr. Binkowski will be here with the others."

"No, not at all," I said. In fact I was relieved not to have to find my way by myself.

"And if she's not home, we can leave a note under her door," said Mrs. Albright. "And tell her where to meet us."

"That sounds perfect," I said.

Chapter 10

I was awake early the next morning. I pulled the drape back a little from the window so I could look down onto the street.

Even at this hour the narrow street was jammed with activity. Trucks stopped in the middle of the street to unload; cars inched around them; bicycles shot through any opening in the traffic that occurred. Pedestrians seemed to weave through the muddle without concern.

I noticed the colors people wore. They were dark and solid: brown, black, dark green. At home people mostly wore brighter colors and prints. I wondered why the difference.

"Jane? What's out there?"

Nella was squinting at the shaft of light I was letting in through the curtains. I closed them again. "Not much," I answered. "Sorry if I woke you."

"What time is it?" came another voice. Anthea's.

"Seven, almost," I said. Anthea groaned and covered her head with her pillow.

"It's time to get up, anyway." Mrs. Albright sounded energetic even first thing in the morning. "Come on, girls—rise and shine!" She snapped on the light. "Does anyone want to use the bathroom before I get in the shower?"

I didn't see how I would get through the day until it was time to see Julia, but I'd reckoned without Mrs. Albright's itinerary.

First we took the subway down to the Battery, which is where you get the ferry boat to the Statue of Liberty. Julia had been right about the subway.

... In the subway I always feel as though I'm wandering among the ruins of Pompeii or Babylon or somewhere. The stations—some of them—must have been beautiful once—there are still fragments of elaborate, beautifully carved archways and pillars, and some of the old, mosaic signs are still there—some even have pieces of gold in them. Passages and stairs snake off in all sorts of directions—it's so mysterious down there. I always run through the subway stations at top speed, as if I'm late, but I must look pretty silly because I never quite know where I'm going and I end up charging up one staircase and down

another, or running around and around the same spot two or three times. Every once in a while I'll work myself into a panic imagining that I'll never find my way out—you see some people in the subway who look as though they've been doomed to spend eternity down there....

The ferry boat was better. We stood in the bow with the breeze on our faces and watched the Statue of Liberty come closer and closer.

Mrs. Albright leaned on the rail next to me. "This makes me feel very close to my grandfather," she said. "So many times he would tell us about seeing the Statue of Liberty for the first time."

Randy Gardiner wanted to walk up all the stairs to the Statue of Liberty's crown, but the rest of us convinced him that it would be better to take the elevator up and walk *down* instead.

I'm glad we did it that way. I'm not sure the view would have been worth the climb. Everything looks small and hazy from up there. I like to be able to appreciate what I'm looking at. It was more fun to look *at* the Statue than *from* it. She reminded me of my Taj, sort of, even though my Taj was smaller than life and she was bigger.

Instead of the subway we took the bus back uptown. We got off the bus at Grand Central Station and walked to St. Patrick's Cathedral. We had our lunch on the steps of the cathedral, buying stuff from the carts that the street vendors pushed around.

"Ew, gross," cried Nella when Mrs. Albright suggested it. Nella's idea of a New York–style lunch was at a restaurant with white tablecloths and waiters.

"Oh, Nella, where's your sense of adventure?" Mr. Binkowski asked, laughing. "This may be the only chance you ever have to buy from a street vendor. I don't think they can push their carts as far as Westminster, Missouri."

"We have ice-cream trucks. That's close enough," Nella pouted. "I don't want to eat anything that's been sitting in a dirty old box for who knows how long."

"Hey, Mrs. Albright," called out Randy Gardiner. "Can I be a street vendor for the career fair?"

I groaned. "Shut up about the career fair, Randy."

"Look, Nella," said Bob Muller, who'd been watching the crowds around the food carts. "New Yorkers put mustard on their pretzels."

Nella's face crinkled in disgust, but the rest of us laughed at her and got some food. A lot of those vendors just sell hot dogs and pretzels, but some have unusual things. I bought a bag of hot chestnuts from one vendor, and a thing like a potato turnover—I don't remember its name—from another one. It was kind of soggy, but it tasted okay. I think part of what made it taste good was the sudden image of Mother that came to me while I was eating it—Mother talking about how sophisticated and elegant New York would make me. Mother would have loved Nella. All Nella had for lunch was mineral water from a bottle that she took the cap off of herself.

Mrs. Albright stood up. "Well, if the rest of you will excuse us," she said. "Jane and I have an appointment."

My breath caught. All day I'd been walking around with Julia's letters in my head, seeing what she'd been describing; it had felt like we were together. I'd sort of—not quite, but almost—forgotten that I'd get to see her in person.

"Now," said Mrs. Albright as we walked away from the group, "do you have that address?"

"It's on Lexington Avenue," I said. I fished in my pocket for the piece of paper I'd written the address on.

"Good," she said. "That's not far."

We walked up Fifth Avenue a few blocks, then turned east.

"It should be right in this block somewhere," said Mrs. Albright.

I followed the numbers on the buildings with my eyes.

Julia's building had one of those Mailboxes and More places on one side of its front and a florist on the other. In between there were wide double doors that led to the apartments. It looked exactly as elegant as she'd said—the doors were heavy dark wood with etched glass panes and gleaming brass hardware.

We walked up the steps and through the doors. Inside were another set of doors, locked, and an intercom system for calling the residents.

"Do you know her apartment number?" asked Mrs. Albright.

"Four twenty-seven."

Mrs. Albright looked at the directory over the intercom. "Hmm. These are all labeled one-A, one-B, and so on."

Just then a woman came out of the building through the locked double doors. "Excuse me," said Mrs. Albright. "Do you happen to know which apartment Julia Gray lives in?"

The woman shook her head. "Sorry."

"She shares it with a girl named Rosie and they're subletting from a guy who works for *Time* magazine and has gone to Europe for a year," I said quickly.

"Sorry," the woman said again. "I don't know anybody like that in the building."

"Apartment four twenty-seven?"

"We're not numbered like that here," the woman said, pushing open the outer doors. "Sorry."

I felt angry. "This is silly. I send letters to her here. She gets them. She *must* be here!"

Mrs. Albright turned around and went back through the double doors. She went into the mail and package shop. I ran after her.

"Excuse me," she said to the young man behind the counter, "do you have a box number four twenty-seven here?"

He scanned the rows of postal boxes on the wall behind him. The store was very brightly lit and the metal faces of the boxes glared in the light. A sign on the wall above the boxes read

ATTENTION POSTAL BOX OWNERS:
EFFECTIVE JANUARY 1 OUTER DOORS
WILL BE LOCKED BETWEEN 1:00 A.M.
AND 6:00 A.M.

"Yes, we do," he said.

"Is it rented?" asked Mrs. Albright.

The young man checked a ledger book on the counter. "Actually, yes, it is. Sorry."

"Can you tell me to whom it's rented?"

The young man hesitated. "Well, I don't know if that's—"

"Is it rented to Julia Gray?"

He relaxed. "Oh, if you're a friend of hers—"

"I'm her sister," I said. "Do you know where I can find her?"

He looked in the ledger book. "Actually, the address here says the Chelsea Hotel."

I felt deflated. "That's old," I said.

"We might check there," Mrs. Albright said. "Who knows? Maybe she's moved back." She took a pen and paper out of her pocket and scribbled. "Just in case we miss her," she said to the man, "could you give this to Julia next time she comes in?"

We took a cab to the Chelsea. The desk clerk there told us that Julia had checked out in February. The forwarding address she left was the one on Lexington Avenue. The one she'd given me.

Chapter 11

"Never mind," said Mrs. Albright briskly. "This is probably just a miscommunication. Didn't you tell me she was enrolled at City College?"

I nodded.

"Well, then, tomorrow we'll go down there and see what's what. Don't worry, Jane." She patted my shoulder.

We went up to the Metropolitan Museum to catch up with the others.

Julia had been there.

. . . You know you're someplace special as soon as you walk through the doors. In the Great Hall, where you come in, the ceilings are so high they're practically lost in the clouds. The doorways are about twenty feet tall and the steps are so wide it seems like a palace built to

*house the giants, which in a way, I guess, is
the truth. . . .*

We found the rest of our group inside the Temple
of Dendur, in the Egyptian wing. Randy was saying
that he didn't see why they spent so much time chisel-
ing out hieroglyphics for a dead guy who wouldn't be
able to see them, anyway. Mr. Binkowski tried to
explain about different cultures having different
ideas of what's important, but Randy just shook his
head.

Anthea ran her fingertips lightly over the glass
that protected the temple walls and said, "You know,
it must have made the living feel good to be able to
do something like this for the one who died. I bet it
made them feel more connected."

Last year Anthea's brother died from leukemia.

After the Egyptian wing we went upstairs, past
the Gallery of Musical Instruments.

A small glass case on a stand, away by itself near
the gallery railing, caught my eye. I went over to look
inside.

I don't know how to describe it, exactly. It was
kind of like a doll house, or one of my birdhouses—
a small replica of a violin maker's studio.

Sawdust was scattered on the floor and tiny tools
lay on the workbenches and the little shelves. Curtains of minutely patterned fabric hung at the windows and lamps no bigger than a quarter hung from
the ceiling. And everywhere there were instru-

ments—violins, guitars, lutes, a balalaika—in varying stages of assembly. Some were hung from the rafters, drying I supposed, and some lay on the benches amid piles of shavings. Some were propped in the corners and were held together with clamps.

A pot of varnish sat open on the stove and there was even a pitcher of water standing on a nearby cabinet.

"Like it?" A dark, young-looking man had come up beside me. "It's a new exhibit; I like to come out and hear what people think of it."

"Did you build this?"

"Oh, no," he said. "It was built about 1830. By a violin maker—a luthier—oddly enough." He grinned. "At least, we think so. We don't know much about it except that it was acquired by a collector in 1927, and then left to us by his widow."

"I love it," I said. "It looks like the violin maker just stepped away. I never thought—"

"Not all of it is entirely to scale," he said. "And the electric lights—I think they must have been added at some later time."

"Yes, but still. It's like seeing a moment from another time."

Mrs. Albright called to me then, and I caught up with the others in the American wing. But nothing for the rest of the day compared to that violin maker's shop.

Chapter 12

The next morning Mr. Binkowski took the rest of the group to the Brooklyn Botanical Gardens, and Mrs. Albright and I went over to City College.

City College doesn't look like a college. At home the college is away from the town and it looks like a park: There are gates at the entranceway and beautiful plants and flowers around the lawns between the buildings. City College is just scattered around the city. I guess they moved in wherever there was space. Once we got inside their administration building, though, it seemed more like a college. I wonder if all colleges smell the same—like paper.

The woman at the desk at the registrar's office had a sour face, wrinkled and tight like an old lemon. She didn't even look up from the book she was reading when we came in.

"Excuse me," said Mrs. Albright.

The woman sighed hugely as though we'd interrupted her at a masterwork. "Yes?"

Mrs. Albright smiled. "I wonder if you could help me," she said. "I'm looking for someone who I think is a student here. Her name is Julia Gray."

"Don't know her."

Mrs. Albright smiled even more nicely. "Could you tell me if she's registered, please?"

The woman sighed again, but she slammed her book shut and turned to her computer terminal. She clattered a few words on the keyboard. "Gray, Julia," she read from the screen. "Hmm."

"What? What is it?"

"There are no grades entered for the midterm. It looks like she stopped going to class in the middle of the term."

I felt a clutch of fear in my stomach.

"Is there an address?" asked Mrs. Albright calmly.

The address was the one for the Chelsea Hotel.

"How about Nicholas Quill?" I said suddenly.

"He's a professor. I can't give you his address."

"Is he at the college today? Can you tell us where we can find him?"

"He's teaching a class now; here in this building, Room three sixty-five. Out at eleven-thirty."

Mrs. Albright looked at her watch. "Almost an hour from now. Let's go get a cup of coffee while we wait, Jane."

There was a small coffee shop across the street from the administration building. We went in and sat down in a booth. Mrs. Albright ordered coffee and a bagel; I asked for a vanilla milk shake. The waiter didn't smile or say thank you or anything. After that Ms. Sour Face it was too much.

"I don't understand these people in New York," I said.

Mrs. Albright cut her bagel into little tiny pieces but I didn't notice that she ate any of it. The hour passed slowly.

The elevator in the college building was out of order so we had to walk up to the third floor. Nicholas Quill came through the door of Room 365 as we approached it. I recognized him from what Julia had said.

He was kind of small and he had an ordinary brown-and-gray beard trimmed close to his jaw, but his eyes made his face seem uncommon. They were dark and liquid-looking. I felt hopeful.

Mrs. Albright introduced us and said, "We're trying to track down one of your students."

"Who are you looking for?"

"A girl named Julia Gray," said Mrs. Albright. "She's enrolled in one of your seminars. About nineteen, blond, very long hair."

"And when would she have been a student of mine?"

I was puzzled. How could he not remember Julia? "Now," I said. "This term."

Nicholas Quill put his briefcase down on the floor of the hallway and pulled a spiral-bound ledger from it. He thumbed through it. "Here," he said. "Elements of Fiction. Yes. But according to my attendance records she hasn't been in class since midterm."

"If you could tell us anything you remember about her, we'd appreciate it," said Mrs. Albright. "Did she seem worried or upset? Frightened at all?"

Nicholas Quill shook his head. "I'm sorry," he said, "but I don't remember anything about her at all." He started to close his briefcase. "There are more than forty people in that class. I can't remember all of them."

"Perhaps if you do remember something, you'll get in touch with us at the Holiday Inn," Mrs. Albright said.

But I wasn't ready to give up. "You must remember her!" I burst out. "She told me you thought she was talented!"

"No," he said definitely. "No. I make it a point to never say that."

"Promising." I said in an accusing voice. "That was the word she said you used."

He shrugged and began to walk away, but I walked with him. Mrs. Albright followed us.

"So how could you not remember her?"

"I don't remember her," he repeated. He walked faster.

"A story she wrote for your class was bought by a magazine!" I said desperately.

He shook his head. "I'm sorry."

I was so angry that my ears began to ring. "How

could you not remember Julia?" My voice echoed in the hallway and others began to look at us curiously.

"Jane," said Mrs. Albright. "Calmly."

I took a deep breath. I tried to calm down. "She thought you were wonderful," I said bitterly.

His eyes darkened. In anger? Pain? He said more gently, "Maybe she wrote more fiction than you knew."

I didn't understand.

"I think I'd remember if someone in one of my seminars sold a story to a magazine," he said.

"What are you saying? That it didn't happen? She didn't sell a story?"

He shrugged again.

Noises on the stairs interrupted us: the clang of metal against metal and a heavy dragging thump. I turned around to look, and through the balusters I saw a boy on crutches. He had a brace around his back and down his legs. He was trying to get up the stairs. His torso was twisted and his left leg stuck straight out at a clumsy angle. To get up the stairs at all he had to go backward, swinging his left leg up to the next highest step before he pushed his body up with the crutches. His face was livid with effort.

He dropped his backpack and it tumbled back all the way down to the landing. Mrs. Albright and I started forward, but another student picked up the bookbag and slung it over her shoulder without even breaking stride. "I'll take it to class for you," she said over her shoulder. He nodded.

Mrs. Albright went down to the boy. "Can I help you somehow?"

He was gasping for breath. "Get them to fix the damn elevator."

"I'll mention it down in the office," she said. She would too. "In the meantime, perhaps—could you be carried up the stairs?"

"*No!*" It was a roar. He poked out the crutch at us as though it were a weapon.

We backed away.

The boy continued his ordeal, swinging his leg then forcing his body up after it. It was painful to watch; I turned aside.

Nicholas Quill couldn't seem to look away. His face was parchment white as he watched. His breath came in the same short, sharp gasps as the boy's. His shoulders twitched as the boy labored.

I knew why Nicholas Quill was upset. He was just like Julia. She always got caught up in other people's struggles—almost as though whatever was happening was happening to her.

At last the boy made it up the steps. Sweat made tails of his hair and his shirt clung to his thin shoulders. He moved away down the corridor without looking in our direction.

Nicholas Quill took a handkerchief from his pocket and mopped his face. He mumbled something unintelligible and went rapidly away down the hall.

"Wait!" I called suddenly, anxiously. "Do you remember a girl coming to class, to that seminar that Julia was in, with a black eye?"

His steps slowed. "Yes, I do. Why?"

Julia would have befriended that girl. Nicholas Quill walked away from what upset him, but Julia got involved.

"Do you know her name?"

He set down his briefcase again, took out his notebook again. "Rosalinda," he answered finally. "Rosalinda Chavez. She doesn't come anymore either."

Rosie.

But the name was a dead end after all. The registrar's office had no address at all for Rosalinda Chavez.

As we went out the front door of the college—we did stop at the office—and down the stairs to the street, I said, "Mrs. Albright, do you think we should go to the police about Julia?"

"I'm not entirely sure." She hesitated. "I wonder if we ought to call your mother."

Mother. "No." I didn't want her to be involved. That would be like a betrayal of Ju.

"She's not home now, anyway," I said. "Let's go talk to the police and see what they say before we call my mother."

Chapter 13

At the police station everything was out in the open. All the partitions along the corridors and between the offices were clear like glass, and frosted windows high up near the ceiling glowed with the light of outdoors. It should have seemed like a light and airy place but instead it felt dark, like a mine. It smelled like sweat.

And it was crowded. A police officer led us through a corridor jammed with people. One cluster of women was all handcuffed together and somebody, I couldn't see who, was screaming horrible things. We went into an office area where it wasn't so crowded, and the officer put two chairs for us near a battered old desk and told us to wait for the detective lieutenant.

Snatches of other people's conversation swirled like smoke in the air above our heads.

"We found the body of the Pagnozzi woman—"

"—and when Lukas went up to her she *bit* him—"

"—a thirty-eight caliber bullet "

When the detective lieutenant finally came, he sat down behind the desk and stared at us for a minute without saying anything. He had dark hair and eyes and very pale skin. His face looked dry and furrowed, as though it had been whittled out of a piece of wood.

"All right," he said. He pulled a typewriter on a rolling stand over to the desk and pulled out a form from a drawer. He rolled the form into the typewriter. "You say you've got a missing person? Your daughter?" He looked at Mrs. Albright.

"No," I said. "My sister."

"Name?"

"Jane," I said. "Jane Gray."

Mrs. Albright said, "I think he means the name of the missing person, Jane. Julia's name."

"Oh." I felt hot. "Sorry."

"Julia," said the detective, typing. "Julia Gray?"

I nodded.

"Address?"

I hesitated.

The detective sighed. "*Her* address."

"I *know*," I flashed, "but that's just it; we don't know. The address we had for her isn't any good."

He pushed the typewriter away and put his elbows on the desk and his chin in his hand. "All right. Just tell me about it."

I did. I told him everything—about all the letters

from Julia, and about writing to her and not getting any answer, and about finding out that her address was a Mailboxes and More. I told him about going to the college to look for her.

He said when I had finished, "Well, I can call the hospitals and the shelters, but I don't think we're going to find anything."

I felt my heart thud. "Then do you think she's been kidnapped or something?"

"No," he hesitated, glanced at Mrs. Albright, then looked back at me. "To be honest with you, I think she disappeared on purpose."

I didn't understand what he meant. "On purpose?"

"I don't think she wants you to find her," he said.

"But—why not?"

"Maybe things weren't going as well for her as she'd led you to believe."

I was incredulous. "How can you call my sister a liar? You don't know anything about her!"

He sighed. "No, I don't know your sister, but I've known hundreds of kids just like her. They come to New York City with their heads full of dreams and their eyes full of stars. They get disappointed. And sometimes, things get bad."

"But that's what I'm talking about—something bad must have happened to my sister."

He shook his head. "You say your sister had money. Then it's not likely she was forced into homelessness or prostitution."

"But what if somebody hurt her?"

"There's no evidence—nothing to suggest that she had any enemies or was in any kind of danger—I know, I know, you've heard lots of stories about the terrible things that happen in New York; but believe me, most violence against persons is done by an acquaintance or relation. But, just in case, like I said I'll check out the hospitals. And the morgues.

"If I were you, though, I'd just give her time. She'll turn up."

"But can't you look for her?"

He shook his head. "She hasn't done anything illegal, we don't have any reason to think she's in danger, and she's not a minor child."

Mrs. Albright nodded her head, reluctantly.

I stood up. "Thank you very much for your time," I said woodenly. I headed for the door without waiting for Mrs. Albright.

She caught up with me in the lobby.

"Do you still think I ought to call my mother?" I asked bitterly. "And tell her what? That everything turned out just the way she thought it would?"

"It's late," said Mrs. Albright. "Let's go back to that coffee shop and have some lunch. Maybe things will look brighter when we've eaten."

She always wants to eat when there's a problem. I've never thought about it before, but Mrs. Albright is fat.

Chapter 14

When we got back to the hotel there was a large bulky envelope waiting for me at the desk. On top of it was clipped a note.

> *Miss Gray:*
> *I happened to find some copies of work that your sister turned in to my seminar. Since she's no longer in my class, I have no further use for them. I thought they might be of some interest to you.*
>
> *Very truly yours,*
Nicholas Quill.

There were maybe a half-dozen papers. On one of them she'd gotten a grade of D. "Trivial," the comment said. The others were spattered with red ink:

Words were circled, whole paragraphs were crossed out, phrases were added. Scrawled observations like "awkward" and "labored" littered the pages.

Now I had to believe it.

Julia had lied to me.

My golden sister.

Chapter 15

We checked with *Time* magazine, of course. Rosie's father didn't work there; no one named Chavez worked there at all.

The others in the group went to a play that night; I wouldn't go.

"Please," I begged Mrs. Albright, "I just want to be by myself for a while." It seemed a century since I'd had any time alone.

After they all left I lay on my rollaway bed and stared out the window.

Loneliness was eating a big hole in my stomach.

I didn't even have my memories of Julia now— everything that people had been telling me made her seem like a stranger. I wondered if I'd ever known her at all.

And I missed Eben. So much. I wished I hadn't made him mad.

There was no one I could talk to. I felt as though there were a pane of glass between me and the rest of the world.

Light from the restaurant across the street spilled into the street when the door opened to admit an elegantly dressed couple. I smiled, sort of; it was quite a change from the morning when delivery vans blocked the street and workmen heaved boxes in and out through the entranceway to the restaurant. A fragment of one of Julia's letter echoed in my mind:

> *The city is different after sunset. The lights come on; they glitter and twinkle above the street like an artificial sky. On the pavement, golden pools spill onto the sidewalk whenever doors open and people pass inside. Only a few pass inside; the rest stay out. It reminds me of prehistoric times, Janey: Safety and warmth are found within the ring of firelight. The dark is dangerous; frightening figures lurk there. It's cold here now, especially at night. . . .*

That was exactly how it looked.

What Julia had written about New York was true, anyway.

True. I sat up.

The detective at the police station was wrong. Nicholas Quill was wrong too. Julia wasn't like they said.

Julia *wasn't* a liar.

And she *was* a good writer.

Relief broke over me like sudden sunlight. How could I have doubted her? Urgently I had to find my sister—I had to tell her I believed in her.

I jumped off the bed ready to do something, then stopped short.

Do what?

I still didn't know where she was.

How do you find a missing person, anyway?

The police wouldn't help.

I didn't know any private detectives.

I thought about flyers on telephone poles and pictures on milk cartons. I thought of the missing-person television shows.

The media.

The newspapers.

I called Tom.

His voice was cheerful. "Jane! How's life in the big city?"

"Tom." My voice sounded wobbly. I steadied it. "Do you know any newspaper people in New York City?"

Immediately he became serious. "What is it, Jane? Is there a problem?"

"Not a problem, really," I said carefully. I didn't want him to talk to Mother about this. "I think I can handle it, anyway. Do you know anybody?"

"Bob Lally's at the *Daily Clarion*. He's an old college friend of mine."

"Do you think he'd mind if I went to see him?"

"No. He's a good guy. Janey? Are you sure you don't want to talk about this?"

"I'm sure. I'll talk to you later, okay?"

Chapter 16

The next morning I went over to the *Daily Clarion*. On my own—I convinced Mrs. Albright that I didn't need a chaperon just to go see an old friend of Tom's, and anyway the Clarion building was only a couple of blocks from the hotel. She let me go by myself; I think she'd started to feel bad about not spending much time with the other kids, anyway.

I walked over, trying to make myself a part of the darkly clothed New York crowd.

There was a globe in the lobby of the Clarion building, the biggest globe I've ever seen. My head only came up to Texas, that's how big it was. It wouldn't even have fit in the lobby if they hadn't taken a scoop out of the floor to accommodate it. When I got close I saw that they'd lined the scoop with mirrors and lamps—it was almost as though the earth was sitting in a bowl of light.

They'd continued the latitude and longitude markings from the globe into the rest of the lobby, putting them in as lines of brass in the dark marble walls and floors. It made me feel as though I were in outer space, looking down at the world from a godly distance.

I went up to the seventh floor and told the guard at the desk in front of the elevators that I wanted to see Mr. Lally. I told him my name and that I was a friend of Tom's. In a minute or so a big, gray-haired man came barreling down the corridor. I didn't have time to get an impression of him—he held out a hand to me as he passed and swept me along with him down the hall.

"We'll have to walk and talk," he said. "How's old Tom doing these days? And what can I do for you?"

"Tom's okay," I said. I tried to be succinct. "I need help to find my sister."

We ran down some stairs to a long low room where rows of people were standing at easel-type desks. I knew this place from Tom's newspaper; it was the paste-up room. I recognized the smell: ink. Somebody brought a page over to Mr. Lally. He pointed out the changes he wanted.

"She came to New York to be a writer. For a while I got letters, but they stopped."

Up the stairs again to the features department. We passed a wall with huge blowups of the paper's prize-winning photographs.

"When I got here I found out that the address I

had for her was no good and now I don't know where she is."

Over to the art department.

"Why did she disappear? And where did she go? I need to know, Mr. Lally. Can you help me?"

"I'll introduce you to Barton Walsh," Mr. Lally said briskly. "He's one of my best reporters."

"I appreciate it—" I started, but he brushed it off.

"Nothing to appreciate," he said. "Sounds like a good story for us. Readers lap up that life-in-the-big-city kind of thing. TV's done it—all those real-life, you-solve-'em shows. We have to compete."

We'd come through a doorway into the city room and were weaving our way through a maze of desks and file cabinets and computer terminals and stacks of newspapers and magazines and books. It was just as cramped and messy as the police station, but for some reason it didn't give me the same feeling of being in the bowels of the planet. I guess because, for one thing, there weren't as many smells.

Without even slowing down Mr. Lally waved me toward a desk. "Bart," he called out. "Talk to this girl. She's got a story for you."

I peered around a stack of newspapers taller than I was.

All I saw of Barton Walsh was his back. He was hunched in front of a video terminal, eyes fixed on the screen and fingers racing across the keyboard.

"Mr. Walsh?"

"One minute, one minute," he threw over his shoulder. The screen flashed and his words disappeared. He shook his shoulders loosely and spun around in his chair to face me. He was thin, with long blond hair and large horn-rimmed glasses that made his eyes look huge. He cocked his head to one side like a curious bird and regarded me brightly. "Call me Bart," he said. "Hi. Sit down." He waved his hand at a chair-height stack of newspapers, and I balanced myself gingerly on it. "Tell me."

I told him what I'd told Mr. Lally.

"Okay," he said. "But I'm going to need more, a lot more. I'm going to have to be able to make your sister live for the readers. Tell me what she's like."

"She's about five-five, she has brown eyes and blond hair, long, down to her waist—"

He interrupted. "No, don't tell me what she *looks* like. Tell me what she *is* like. Get it?"

I got it. "Well," I began, "she sort of—shines." That sounded dumb. I'm not great at describing things; Julia's the word person.

"I have her letters," I said finally. "Do you want to read them?"

"Letters?"

"Yes. Julia wrote to me nearly every day until I wrote and told her I was coming to New York."

"And you brought them all with you?"

"Well, not here. They're at the hotel."

"It would be great if I could read them. You're sure you don't mind?"

Barton walked back to the hotel with me and waited while I went upstairs. I brought the letters down and handed them to him, but he said, "No, I'd like to read them with you around so you can answer questions if I have any. Do you mind?"

"No." We settled into two of the big squashy chairs that decorated the lobby, with the letters in a pile on my lap.

I unfolded one and handed it to him.

He scanned it. "She knows how to turn a phrase, anyway. Tell me about this thing between Julia and your mother."

I shrugged. "It's hard to explain if you don't know her. Mother, I mean."

"Is she always on your case?"

"Not exactly." I hesitated. "She has these—standards—she expects us to live up to."

"And Julia, being a writer, wasn't living up to standards?"

"No. Mother didn't think Julia would be a success."

Barton said, "Too bad. It's hard enough to make it these days; it's twice as tough without your family behind you."

We were silent for a while. Barton read with complete concentration. He didn't even look up when the hotel porter ran the vacuum cleaner under his chair.

"I like these descriptions of the city. Have you been to some of the places she described?"

"Yes."

"So you know."

After a while longer he said, "I like your sister."
He read one of the letters out loud.

Dear Janey:

*I took one of my usual wrong turns in the
bowels of the subway system and ended up in
a dead end. At first I thought it was an old
abandoned station—there were piles of big old
cardboard boxes and other refuse everywhere.
Everything looked damp and greasy and the
smell down there was indescribable.*

But I heard singing.

*It wasn't a good voice or anything; just a
high droning sound, but it surprised me. I'd
thought I was the only person within miles—
like in that story "By the Waters of Babylon,"
do you remember? The sound seemed to be
coming from the pile of boxes. I moved closer,
and then, in a rip in one of the boxes. I saw
eyes. For a minute I thought they were my
own; that I was looking into a fragment of steel
or an old broken mirror, and then I realized
there was a person in there—*

I shuddered. I didn't want to think about Julia
down there amid the boxes and the smell.

"I think this will make a good story," said Barton.
"Can I keep these letters? No, of course not"—seeing
my face—"stupid of me. But how about if I make
copies of them; would that be all right?"

88

"Oh, yes!"

"Good." He gathered them together. "I'll take them with me now and then send them back over here tonight."

"When will the story be in the paper?"

"Oh, I don't know. I'll need a few days to work on it, then it'll be up to editorial to schedule it. Could be a couple of weeks."

"But I'm leaving the day after tomorrow!"

"Don't worry. Just leave me your home address and phone number. Anybody who has any information will call the paper anyway, not you. I'll pass it on."

"But I was hoping I could find her—see her—before I left."

He patted my shoulder. "Don't worry, kid."

Easy for him to say.

Chapter 17

"Jane."

Mrs. Albright was alone in the room when I went upstairs. "Jane, sit down.

"I called your mother," she said.

I couldn't believe it. "Why?"

"She had a right to know."

"Why?"

Mrs. Albright was patient. "She's your mother. And Julia's. She cares."

Now Mother would know how badly Julia had failed.

"She and Mr. Easley are coming in on the first flight in the morning."

The rest of the afternoon was misery. Mrs. Albright and Mr. Binkowski took us to Central Park to see the zoo. I wasn't impressed. The zoo in St. Louis is better and it isn't nearly so far away. And we took hansom cab rides around the park. Nella lapped it up, pretending to be Mrs. Rockefeller or somebody. I hate Nella.

I waited in the hotel lobby for Mother and Tom. They arrived exactly when I expected them to. Mother was wearing her red wool suit and a pin that looked like the Victoria Cross or something.

Tom turned away from the registration desk and saw me. He grinned. "Janey!"

"Hi, Tom. Hello, Mother." I kissed her cheek.

"Hello, Jane. We didn't expect you to wait for us. You should have gone out with your class."

"Yes, Mother, but I thought—"

She handed me her carry-on bag and headed toward the elevator. She had her stone face on—it hadn't registered a single emotion since she'd entered the hotel.

But I wasn't going to let her intimidate me. "—the quicker I could bring you up-to-date the quicker we could accomplish something," I finished.

As Tom and Mother unpacked I told them what had happened since I talked to Tom on the phone.

"I don't know when the piece will appear in the paper," I finished, "but I think it'll help when it does."

"Well, we can't wait," said Mother abruptly. "We'll have to hire a private detective. It's what should have been done in the first place. If you had called me—"

I was speechless. For the last four months she'd practically pretended she didn't even have an older daughter. How was I supposed to know that she'd be so concerned?

"Fine," I said sarcastically. "Hire a private detective. Know one? What are you going to do, look one up in the yellow pages?"

"We'll get referrals," she answered coolly. "I'll call that police detective you spoke to and ask him to recommend somebody."

I felt myself fading under the glare of her personality, the way a photograph does when it's left in the sun. I hated my mother so much at that moment I didn't even want to be in the same room with her. "I'm going to my room," I muttered sullenly and got up to leave.

Tom followed me to the door. "Janeybird, you did good," he said, patting me on the shoulder. "That was a smart idea, to get in touch with the newspaper."

"It was more than you did," I said nastily. "Thanks for all your support. You didn't say two words in there."

I sagged against the elevator wall as the door slid shut behind me. I felt bad about how mean I'd been to Tom; I also felt bad about how mean Mother had been to me.

Julia wasn't the only one out there alone someplace. It seemed like every person in the family was cut adrift and sinking fast.

By six o'clock that evening the three of us were in

the hotel bar, sitting across a table from the retired police detective the lieutenant had suggested. Mother had been in New York City for all of five hours. Whatever else you could say about her, you had to admit she was efficient.

The detective was paunchy and bald. He had the same expression in his eyes that the lieutenant had had—wary, tired. I already knew what he'd say.

"Lady," he said, after Mother had finished explaining, "I've got to tell you, it'd be a waste of my time and your money to look for someone who doesn't want to be found."

"I'm not purchasing your opinion," Mother said coldly. "I'm purchasing your services. Do you want the job or not?"

"Oh, I'll take it," he answered, shrugging, "just so's you understand the odds up front. And, you understand, even if I do find her, there's no guarantee she'll want to talk to you. And I can't make her. I can tell you where she is, and I can tell her you want to get in touch, but that's all. You understand?"

"We understand," said Tom drily.

Mother wrote out a check for his retaining fee and the investigator put it in his pocket.

"Julia is better off than most," Tom reminded Mother and me. "She has financial resources."

The investigator nodded. "These kids come here all the time. They're more practical than you'd think from their ideas. They work as waiters or word processors or whatever until they get bored and go home."

94

"Or until their big break comes," I amended. He shrugged.

"She did tell me she was going to look for some sort of a job," I remembered.

The investigator nodded. "She's probably holed up somewhere licking her wounds. I wouldn't worry."

As the investigator made his way out of the bar, Mother seethed. "Idiot!"

"I thought he was pretty sound," said Tom.

"Telling us so cheerfully not to worry. Idiot! Let one of his kids disappear—let's see him not worry. Idiot!"

I'd never seen Mother so close to losing control. Her face was red and she was shaking.

"Elaine, now take it easy. This guy must know what he's talking about. He's had more experience with these kinds of things than we have." Tom looked at me.

"Yes," I said obediently. "He made me feel better."

But I wasn't sure that was true. The thing was, I wasn't sure how practical Julia was. With my mind's eye I see her that night on the railroad bridge— high up on the struts, arms held out wide, the breeze streaming back her white blond hair. Everyone else on the bridge steps carefully, looks down at what their feet are doing, but Julia's head is tilted up— she has her eyes on the sky and she practically dances across the beam, laughing, laughing. She doesn't care what's swirling around beneath her. She doesn't even see it.

Chapter 18

After dinner we walked up Broadway toward the theater district.

Times Square at night is different from Times Square during the day. So many people. I found myself trying to look in the faces of every one of them, thinking that maybe by some miracle I'd see Julia. Sometimes I'd only catch a glimpse of a face before the crowd closed in front of me like a tide.

There was one woman wearing a pink, shiny too-short spandex skirt and silver high heels without any hose. There was a tattoo of a spider above her left breast. Her eyes were slate flat and black.

A boy with a bright red ball cap turned wrong way around on his head was hunkered down on the pavement with a pack of cards in front of him, calling a patter like a carnival barker. I couldn't understand what he said. Another man in a suit of purple fur with a dozen gold chains or more around his neck was standing in an entryway, shouting. A woman was leading what might have been a lion on a leash. She was singing.

And there were tattered, stinking homeless women with five coats on, their lives in square paper sacks on the ground beside them. Too many of these to count. One of them leaned up against Tom and reached up her clawed fingers in raveled gloves to his face; she was talking, spit drooling down, begging. I saw Tom hand her some bills.

Most of these women and the men like them were sick, someone had told me. Unstable. Emotionally, mentally ill.

How stable was Julia, after Nicholas Quill had not liked her writing, after her dream had been killed?

By the time we got to the theater, none of us was in the mood for a show. We took a cab back to our hotel.

Chapter 19

Go home, they told us. There's nothing more for you to do here. Live your lives. We'll be in touch if there's any lead on Julia.

So that's what we did.

Nobody said a word during the long drive home from the airport. The house was dark when we pulled up. We went in through the back door, and Mother turned on the lamp over the breakfast table. It made an island of light in the shadows.

"Chilly," she said. "Does anyone else want hot chocolate?" She got out milk and a saucepan.

She seemed so calm. I thought about what Barton Walsh had said, about Mother not thinking that Ju would be a success. This whole mess was her fault. If she had only believed in Julia, Ju would still be at home with us, in her own room, writing at her own desk—

I boiled over. I picked the saucepan up off the stove and just threw it. Milk pooled on the floor and dripped from the cabinets. Flecks of cocoa clung to Mother's pearls.

" 'Does anyone want hot chocolate?' " I mimicked. "You make me sick! Your daughter is who knows where—she may be sick or probably hurt somewhere and you can't even spare a thought! Act like a human being for once in your life!"

She didn't move a muscle.

I went on mercilessly. "She could be dead, did you think of that?" I wanted Mother to hurt; I wanted to make her feel the way I imagined Julia was feeling.

"Maybe it would be better if she were." Mother picked up a dish towel and slowly began to blot her sweater.

Her words shocked me to my core. "You can't mean that!"

She sat down at the breakfast table, closed her eyes, sighed. "I am so tired," she said in a tone that I'd never heard from her before. "I did try; I tried so hard; but I'm so tired now. I can't do anything more."

"Elaine . . . ," said Tom, reaching out his hands to cover hers. "It's all right, you've done a wonderful job."

She went on in that same thin voice. "Don't you understand, Jane? It hurts so much to hope. Dreams always die."

I hadn't thought my mother had ever had a dream in her life.

"Even after you girls were born, I kept on with my watercolors," she said. "I thought that someday . . . but your father didn't know what it meant to me. He just thought it was cute that I'd hung one of my own paintings over the living room fireplace. Once, when we had company, he started to tease me about my pictures. . . ."

She was silent, remembering. After a moment, she continued in a softer voice. "And then, your father and I had such plans, such hopes for the family, for you girls. But those dreams died too. Suddenly I was all alone with two children and a house to take care of. You needed to be safe. That was the important thing. Keep them safe, your father said. I tried. I did try. Tom, didn't I?"

"You did," he said soothingly. "And you succeeded."

It was as though someone had turned on a tap and let all the strength run out, draining away from her.

"It's important for children to have strong parents." She went on. "And there was the insurance money for you, so that you could go to college—I thought you would always be safe. The insurance money was supposed to make you safe."

She laughed, sort of; it sounded awful. "But if it hadn't been for that insurance money, Julia would never have been able to leave. I tried to stop her. I tried everything I knew. It hurts. I guess she knows that now."

She looked at me shyly. "I used to read her letters

101

too, you know. I'd look for them in your room when you were at school. At least I knew she was all right, even if she hated me. I hope you don't mind."

She began to cry.

Tom put his arms around her and took her up to her room.

I couldn't stop shaking. I sat down at the breakfast table and pressed my hands between my legs, but I couldn't stop shaking.

Chapter 20

The sun was warm on my face; I woke up. The comfort and familiarity of my own old bed surprised me. I'd been dreaming about the New York subway system.

I went to the window. The flowers in the garden were crayon-bright in the sunlight. My birdhouses looked cheery. In the Blakes' backyard Eben was mowing the lawn. The old push mower he always used purred as it rolled across the grass. It all looked like a picture.

I'd been home for over a week, and Eben hadn't been over once. I wondered if he even knew that I had gone away.

I pulled on some sweats and went downstairs. No one was around; that was a relief. I poured myself a cup of coffee and sat down at the breakfast table.

The phone rang.

"Did you get them?" It was Barton, calling from New York.

"Get what?"

"The tear sheets of the story. Julia's story. It was in Sunday's magazine section. I sent them out overnight mail yesterday."

There was a knock at the door. "Hang on, I think they just came."

"Call me back after you've read it. Things are popping. The wire services picked up the story. Do you know what that means? It'll be in newspapers all over the country."

"Good for you!"

"Good for Julia," he corrected, and hung up.

A FABLE OF NEW YORK

Once upon a time, from a little town deep in midwestern America, a young girl named Julia Gray set out to seek her fortune. She wanted to be a novelist, and New York, she knew, was the place to come to do it. All her life she had imagined living in the great city: taking seminars from famous authors, meeting publishers at cocktail parties, having lunch at the Algonquin. She'd watched all the movies and read all the books and promised herself she'd follow in the footsteps of Fitzgerald and Wolfe, Hemingway and Salinger, E. B. White and James Thurber.

So, in the fullness of time, she came to New York.

She loved the city, and she wrote to her sister about it . . .

Here Barton had put in some of Julia's letters; the ones about what the city was like.

. . . and in the beginning it seemed as though her dream were coming true . . .

And here were all the letters about the seminar and moving to the apartment and selling her story and everything.

. . . But then something happened. Julia's little sister decided to come to New York to visit Julia.

Then Julia stopped writing letters home.

And when her sister came to visit, Julia was nowhere to be found. The *Northeastern Review* has no record of her short story. There is no trace of Rosie, and no apartment. Nicholas Quill doesn't remember having her in his class, although records do indicate that she was there, at least for a while. Julia did leave some papers behind; papers that indicate that perhaps her gift did not shine as brightly in New York as it had in Westminster, Missouri.

Where is Julia? There are no answers, there are only questions. The police have no report; she doesn't appear to have committed a crime or been the victim of one. The shelters haven't seen her, and neither have the morgues.

And who is Julia? Is she a liar?

Remember, she came to New York to learn to write fiction.

Perhaps she's found a way into that *other* New York, the one that exists in shadowy parallel to our own prosaic lives—the New York City of legend, mythology, and dream.

We don't know. The only trace of Julia we can find is in her letters home.

Unless, of course, you've seen her. There are probably thousands of her in this city.

I felt like crying.

He'd printed all of Julia's letters. That wasn't what I'd wanted. He was supposed to write *about* her, not expose her like that.

Now Julia would be the one to be ridiculed.

I didn't want Mother to see this. All our lives she'd been protecting us, now I was protecting her. I didn't want her to be a witness to Julia's humiliation. I took the clippings up to my room and hid them under my mattress.

Chapter 21

The next day at breakfast there was a letter by my place, from Ms. Owens at the Missouri State Library. It was an invitation to the opening night party for the exhibit.

I'd almost forgotten about the exhibit. I wandered down to my workshop. It looked dusty and neglected. I went back up to my room and flopped down on the bed.

I thought of my mother and the way they'd laughed at her paintings. I thought of Julia's letters in all the papers. The thought of my little birdhouses on display for everyone to see made my face burn.

But it was too late to back out.

Opening night for the exhibit was warm. The breeze from the river brought close the calls of the river boats: the sweet calliope hoots of the dinner cruisers and the stout strong voices of the tows. I wanted to go out there, I wanted to float down the river on the deck of a boat and feel the soft warm air wash over me. I wanted to be anywhere but at the capital.

The festive lights of the capitol were bright against the darkening sky. Streams of people headed up the long flight of stairs to the entry. The huge bronze doors stood open, spilling light out into the night.

Mother had gotten me a new dress for the occasion, a dark red taffeta. I felt like I was wearing a costume.

Ms. Owens met us just inside the doors. She gave us name tags and programs and told us where the refreshments were. I put my name tag in my bag and she laughed. "Don't be so shy, Jane. I'm going to introduce you during my welcome speech, you know."

I hadn't known. Tom put his arm around my shoulders and gave me a hug.

Glass display cases and screens for hanging pictures made a labyrinth of the rotunda. I saw some pieces of weaving and some pottery and paintings and drawings and photographs. There were some magazines open to stories and poems, and a TV set with a videotape playing. There was music in the background; my program said it was a tape of the St. Louis Youth Symphony playing a piece by a young Missouri composer.

I didn't know where my little birdhouses had been set up, so it was a surprise when I rounded a corner and saw them in a case all by themselves. I'd sent Ms. Owens a lot of them and told her to pick what she wanted, but she'd put them all on display. Some of them were hanging, some sitting on shelves. They'd put some background paper in the case with trees and sky and birds.

There was a small, round-looking man studying my birdhouses. I felt my face flush when he looked up at me.

"Are these yours?"

"Yes."

"Very nice. Very nice indeed."

"Thanks."

"Ever thought of being a model maker?"

A what? "No."

He handed me a card and waved his hand toward the Museum Hall, off to one side of the Rotunda. "Go see what you think."

He moved away.

I headed toward the archway that led into the museum.

There were dozens of models. There was a replica of a French homestead from when Missouri was first settled, a little schoolhouse from the 1930s, and a huge panorama on the history of river travel. That one was my favorite. It showed a winding stretch of the Mississippi. The water looked deep, translucent, practically wet—I don't know how they did that—and the bluffs towered above it. On one curve of the river were boats from the earliest times a dugout canoe like the Indians used, tie-rafts, a keelboat. Around the next curve was a stern-wheel steamboat—with cargo, and passengers—and a snag boat. Around the final curve a modern tow boat pushed loaded barges down the channel.

Three little children were mesmerized by the boats. They had their noses pushed right up against the glass.

"Mom, look! Cows on the boat!"

"Mom, look! What is that, all those rafts tied together. How'd they steer?"

"With poles."

"Poles? Wow."

I looked at the card the short man had handed me. He was an instructor in model building at Bemidji State University.

Ms. Owens's voice came over the public-address system. It was time to be introduced.

I stood on the dais with all the other young Missouri artists (except for the symphony). It wasn't as bad as I thought it would be. Ms. Owens said our names, we bowed, the audience clapped. The governor made a speech.

When I got home I put the man's card in a drawer of my desk and tried to forget about it. I didn't want to think about being a model maker. I didn't want to reach for a dream, like Julia.

She was always in my heart, like an ache. The only times I could really forget about missing her were when I read over her letters. I knew them all practically by heart now; the paper was getting thin on the folds and they were starting to tear.

110

Chapter 22

It used to be I liked waking up in the morning. I would leave my shades open at night so that the sun would wake me up first thing. Now the only thing I thought about in the morning was how long it would be before I could go back to sleep. One Sunday I didn't even get out of bed until two o'clock in the afternoon. Of course, it was raining that day so I didn't have that stupid sun to contend with.

There was a lot of career-planning junk on my desk; a draft of our career-fair project was due next Monday. I might as well be an actuary, I thought. At least I won't have to go very far to do research.

Mother and I had been very gentle with one another since the night we got home from New York. I guess we're closer—I don't think of her as some stone goddess anymore—but somewhere inside I feel as though I've lost something. Now that I know her secrets, why she acts the way she does, I feel responsible for her. I feel like I have to take care of her, protect the vulnerable parts.

And there's no one left to take care of me.

The doorbell rang. I pulled on a pair of sweats and clumped down the stairs.

It was the Federal Express man. He looked like a commercial standing there in his crisp uniform, all clean-cut and scrubbed looking. He had a big box in his arms.

"Ms. Jane Gray?"

"Yes?" I'd never in my life gotten anything by Federal Express.

"Sign on this line, please."

I signed and took the box into the living room. The return address on it was for the *Daily Clarion*.

It was full of letters. A huge big pile of letters. A note on the top said, "Jane. Thought you'd like to see these. Bart."

Most of the letters were addressed to Barton, but some were written to Julia. I picked up one. It was on a page torn from a notebook.

. . . I wanted to be a dancer when I came to New York—a gypsy in Broadway shows. It was a long time ago, but Julia's letter about the bus trip brought it all back. How excited I was! But the auditions scared me. It got to the point where I'd throw up before each one. Once I even threw up during one, and that

was the end of the line for me. I work in a department store now. Not a day goes by that I don't wonder what my life would be like if I'd only had the guts. . . .

And another one:

. . . I wanted to be a race car driver. Now I drive a bus. It's a good living. Everyone has dreams when they're young. Julia ought to grow up. . . .

I heard the back door open. "Mother, come look at these," I called. I forgot that we'd been kind of shy with each other since that night.

. . . I think she's too humiliated to come home. It's too bad our society always categorizes attempts like Julia's in terms of "success" and "failure." She had the courage to try, that's the important thing. If she were my daughter I'd be proud of her. . . .

There were hundreds of letters. One person even said she was Julia, but the handwriting was all wrong and the person didn't even know how to spell. Some of the writers thought Julia was a spoiled brat, but most of them liked her.

. . . I did the same thing when I was Julia's age. I lived in a studio apartment in Greenwich Village with three other guys. My big dream was to write something that the New Yorker *would buy. Eventually I got married, got a job, and had six kids. Dreams change as you grow older, but I'm always glad that I had that time in the Village. . . .*

. . . Julia made me remember what it was like to have a dream. Not a particularly comfortable memory. One thing though, if you can survive this city, you can survive anything. . . .

. . . You have to have the hide of a rhinoceros to get along as a writer with all the rejection they get; but if you're that insensitive to how other people think and feel, you probably can't write anything that would touch anyone else. Julia's weakness is her talent. . . .

Funny thing: Lots of people said that they saw Julia. When I was there I hadn't been able to find her, but now she was everywhere, all over the city.

"What's going on?"

Mother and Tom had come in. They were staring at the letters heaped all over the living room floor. "What is all this, Jane?"

I held up two handfuls of letters. I didn't know

what to say. I'd never told them about Barton's article. "Letters to Julia," I said helplessly.

Mother sank to her knees amid the piles. "What?" She picked some up and began to look through them.

I explained about the article. About how angry I'd been that he'd printed Julia's letters, and about how the wire services had picked up the story.

I looked at Tom. "Well, you should have seen the story at your office. Didn't you?"

"No," he answered. "Not that I always see everything, but someone should have noticed the hometown connection. There will be explanations on Monday, I think." He sat down cross-legged on the floor and began to read the letters.

We spent the whole afternoon on the letters. When we'd read them all and stacked them on the floor by the desk, Mother said, "Julia would love these. We'll save them for her."

Tom said, "Julia would have loved seeing her *own* letters in the newspaper. And, Jane, it was all thanks to you. Do you realize that now she's been published?"

"Thanks to me? But I thought it was terrible that they spread her all out in the newspaper like that. It was so embarrassing to read about everything she'd hoped for, and know that it all had been worthless."

"But it wasn't worthless, don't you see? Look at these letters! Her writing touched thousands of people! That's what she wanted all along!"

I thought of something else. "But that Nicholas Quill. He's supposed to be so great. How could he have been so wrong about Julia? And how could he have been so cruel if he knew how sensitive she was? He must have known that."

"Maybe he thought he was helping her thicken her skin. Like that one letter said—writers have to have a way to deal with criticism," Mother said thoughtfully.

"Or," said Tom, "maybe he just didn't care for her style. But other people did. It's always subjective. In writing or painting or anything else." He looked pointedly at my mother, and she smiled shyly.

I was trying to think what all of this meant. Julia successful; she doesn't have to be ashamed to face us—

We must all have been thinking the same thing. In unison we all looked toward the telephone and waited expectantly.

Chapter 23

I walked home from school this afternoon. It had rained all morning, but now the sun was out and I could smell the blooms of lilac and irises. The scent was exhilarating; it made me want to reach out and gather up wonderful things in my arms.

Last night an editor from New York had called. She said that she and her publishing house wanted to bring out Julia's letters in book form. They would make the official announcement about it today.

A book. Julia would be over the moon.

We still hadn't heard from her; but now it would only be a matter of time, I was sure. Newspapers are maybe kind of transitory, but books are permanent. Maybe Julia hadn't seen the newspaper, but I knew she couldn't miss the book.

Julia's dream was alive.

The thought made me feel good. Better than good. Content.

I still wait for the phone to ring, though. Every time it does, there's a still, small hope inside me that, this time, it's going to be Julia.

Today had been the day for the career fair. I got an *A* on my project. I'd thrown out all that stuff about insurance companies and done model making instead.

The mail was in the box when I got home. Bills for Mother, some magazines, and a course catalog from Bemidji State for me. Bemidji's in Minnesota; it gets cold there. I'd have to get a warmer jacket for the winter.

I changed into my cutoffs and went out to weed the garden.

Eben was mowing his lawn. The purring sound brought back the memories of every happy summer I'd ever had. I leaned over the hedge.

"Hi."

He looked up. "Hi!" He wiped his face with the bottom of his T-shirt. "Congratulations on your show."

"Thanks." I wished he had been there with us. I wished I had invited him.

"I'm glad they put up your King Arthur's Castle. That one's always been my favorite."

"You saw it!"

"Of course I did. Jefferson City isn't so far away."

"But I didn't see you!"

"I didn't go to the reception. That was only for

you celebrities. Mom and I drove down yesterday afternoon."

"Oh."

There was a pause.

"Did you go into the state museum at all?" I asked.

"No, we missed that. Gosh, I haven't been in the museum since they took us there in fourth grade."

"Maybe we can drive down there together sometime," I said. "There's some neat stuff to see."

Eben raked the hair back from his eyes and smiled at me. "It's a date," he said.

I smiled. "It's a date. Want some lemonade, Eben?"

As we walked toward the house together, I reached for his hand and curled my fingers inside his.

The phone was ringing as we came through the door.